Agustín Fernández Paz
WINTER LETTERS

Published in 2015 by
SMALL STATIONS PRESS
20 Dimitar Manov Street, 1408 Sofia, Bulgaria
You can order books and contact the publisher at
www.smallstations.com

This book was first published in the Galician language as Cartas de inverno by Edicións Xerais de Galicia (Vigo, 1995; revised edition, 2007). The series GALICIAN WAVE: The Way of Fiction exists to showcase the best of Galician young adult fiction in English.

More information about Agustín Fernández Paz can be found on the author's website, www.agustinfernandezpaz.gal.

This work received a grant from the General Secretariat of Culture of the Ministry of Culture, Education and University Planning of the Xunta de Galicia in the call for translation grants of the year 2014.

Esta obra recibiu unha axuda da Secretaría Xeral de Cultura da Consellería de Cultura, Educación e Ordenación Universitaria da Xunta de Galicia na convocatoria de axudas para a tradución do ano 2014.

ISBN 978-954-384-041-0

Winter Letters

Agustín Fernández Paz

Translated from Galician by **Jonathan Dunne**

 Small Stations Press

For my nephews Fernando and Xulio and niece Antonia

For I have likewise gazed in sleep
on things my memory scarce can keep.

H. P. Lovecraft, 'To a Dreamer'

1

Tareixa Louzao's eyes lit up when she read the name of the sender on the thick padded envelope the postman had just given her. Seeing written there the name of her brother she hadn't heard from in almost two months lifted a burden from her. She'd been surprised by such a delay since Xabier, wherever he might be, even during the long time he spent in Quebec, never let more than two weeks go by without calling her or dropping her a line, even just a postcard. They'd been very close since they were children, despite the difference in age, and the bond between them, rather than loosening, had grown stronger with the passage of time.

Almost without realizing, she glanced at the photographs on top of the sideboard and remembered the joke Xabier always made when he came to visit and saw the group of framed photographs arranged like the jumbled pieces of a puzzle: 'How is the pantheon of family memories?' Once again she went over these images that preserved some of the most important moments in her life: with her brother and parents in the garden of the family home; with Xabier on what must have been her thirteenth birthday; Xabier signing books, surrounded by people eager to get a dedication; with her mother sitting on the terrace, the summer before she died…

As on other occasions, Tareixa's eyes were drawn to the photo with her between Adrián and Xabier in front of the small chapel on St Roch's Mount. She remembered the day that photo had been taken, during the August festivities. She had just turned sixteen and felt she had the whole of her life in front of her. How distant that memory now seemed! It was that summer when Adrián and Xabier first began to take her with them on their excursions; this was something she loved, there was no one in whose company she felt better. It was also then Tareixa discovered, almost without realizing, something she must have known for quite some time: she was hopelessly in love with Adrián and, despite the twists and turns of fate, that love would remain with her throughout her life.

She shook her head energetically, as if to drive away the sadness she always felt when thinking about Adrián, and looked at the envelope again. The sender's address indicated that Xabier was back in Galicia, though to begin with Tareixa was unable to recognize the place written under her brother's name: Doroña, Vilarmaior. Wasn't that somewhere near Monfero, by the river Eume? I'll have a look on the map, she thought while opening the padded envelope. She was expecting to find a recent publication of her brother's, or copies of a translation of one of his books. Xabier always remembered that Tareixa liked to keep a sample of everything he published, even if, as often happened, it was written in a language she didn't know.

But the contents of the envelope were different from before. Inside was another, similar envelope, slightly smaller than the one she'd just opened, accompanied by two sheets covered in her brother's tiny handwriting. The second envelope was closed, and the flap had been reinforced by thick adhesive tape, as if to protect the contents. Tareixa placed both envelopes on the table, sat down in a chair and prepared to read the message Xabier had sent her.

Dear Tareixa,

Forgive me for writing a few, short lines, and not a longer letter, as you must have expected. You'll be surprised I don't mention what I've been up to these last few weeks, but I've something much more urgent to tell you. You know very well you're the only person in the world I can fully trust, which is why I'm writing to you now, to ask for two favours without having to explain myself any further.

The first is that you absolutely do not open the envelope with this letter. I know it's an unusual request, but I'm sure you'll understand I have good reason to make it.

The second will surprise you, but you know I wouldn't ask this if it wasn't absolutely necessary. If you see, a week after receiving this letter, that I still haven't contacted you by phone, go to the central police station in Vigo and ask for Inspector Soutullo. Tell him you're my sister and hand him the envelope I'm sending you. Do not hesitate, Soutullo is a good friend of mine. We were in close contact three years ago, when I spent some months there carrying out research to write The Defeat of Hope; *I think I may even have introduced him to you. I'm sure Soutullo will pay close attention to the contents of the envelope and will know what to do.*

I ask you not to open the envelope, but I can't stop you also finding out its contents if you're obliged to hand it over to Soutullo. Though, for your own good, I would ask you not to do this, I can't bear the pain you would feel. Do you remember our first trip to Barcelona, in the autumn of 1969? You'll remember that was when I bought Tales of the Cthulhu Mythos *from a kiosk on the Ramblas. It was the first book by Lovecraft I read, his tales fascinated me. Seeing my enthusiasm, you would say you didn't know how I could read those stories you disliked so much. I always answered it was normal you didn't like them, because you made the mistake of believing what they told could be real, when they were just clever inventions that played with our fears. Well, now, as I'm writing to you, from madness or a nightmare, from an unreal world or this village in Vilarmaior, I have to tell you Lovecraft may have been right, you may have been right, and there are things in this world we may not even be able to imagine.*

But it's also possible that everything I'm writing is just the product of a strange nightmare that won't leave me alone. It's possible that in a few days the two of us will be together again, laughing at these lines and the contents of the envelope I'm sending you. Or perhaps, dear sister, what your eyes are reading will be the last words I ever write.

Now, as I finish this letter, I'm aware I also could get away from here and return to the real world, I'm still in time to escape this awful situation. But that would mean abandoning Adrián to his fate, refusing to heed the message he sent me. And I can't do that, especially after reading the letter, or whatever it is, I just found downstairs. I don't know why I'm telling you this when I swore never to give you cause for worry, because to understand what I'm telling you you'd have to read the papers inside the envelope. I would prefer you not to, but you're my sister and I can't prevent you from reading them when the time comes, if that is your wish. Perhaps then you'll understand why, in these final hours, anxiety and fear course through my body.

Farewell, dear sister. I embrace you with all my strength, and hope it's not for the last time.

Xabier

Tareixa's face grew darker as she read the letter, and she began to feel deeply concerned. What was Xabier trying to tell her? What was the purpose of these unsettling references to Adrián? And why these allusions to Lovecraft, the author of those novels – so many years ago! – Xabier devoured with passion and she could never finish? Was it just a joke her brother was playing on her, he who had such a way with words? But her heart was telling her what she'd just read was something more than a literary exercise, and in the coming days she would have to live with the fear she now felt inside.

Over the next two days, Tareixa tried to lead a normal life. While she was in the health centre, overwhelmed by the amount of work she had, she managed to forget Xabier's letter. But as soon as she arrived home and saw the sealed envelope lying on the sideboard, her brother's words came back to mind and a sense of unease took hold of her with ever greater intensity. Why didn't Xabier trust her? And why did he trust this stranger, Soutullo, when he had so many friends in Vigo? Everything seemed to indicate that Xabier and Adrián were involved in some murky incident, maybe that was why he didn't want her to intervene. But what if she paid him attention and waited for seven days, and something happened to them?

The idea of opening the envelope may have worked its way into her mind as soon as she'd finished reading her brother's letter. The two days that had passed may have served only to allow the idea to grow, to grow until it became unbearable. On the third day, unable to take any more, Tareixa decided to ignore her brother's request. It was Saturday, she had the whole day free, and the possibility of spending the whole weekend thinking about Xabier and the contents of the envelope was too much for her. She couldn't wait for so many days to go by, Xabier should never have asked this of her. If it came to it and he rebuked her for being impatient, she could always say it was really his fault, since she'd only opened the envelope because the contents of his letter had worried her so much.

She picked up the sealed envelope and turned it over in her hands, trying to guess what might be inside. It seemed to contain only papers, perhaps it was just a new manuscript of her brother's. After a moment's hesitation, she cut the adhesive tape with a pair of scissors, tore the flap and opened the envelope. She emptied its contents on to the table and examined them closely. There were a few sheets covered in Xabier's unmistakably small, neat handwriting. There were also several letters, all of them addressed to the post office box her brother had in Santiago de Compostela; the envelopes had been opened, so the letters had clearly been read. Tareixa's heart started beating more quickly when she recognized the handwriting that meant so much to her. The sender was always the same, Adrián Novoa, though the addresses the letters had been sent from were different. Some of them came from abroad, but most bore the same address she'd seen in Xabier's letter: Doroña, Vilarmaior. There was also a smaller, padded A5 envelope containing numerous photographs. Tareixa glanced at them quickly and was surprised to see that they were all very similar, as if they belonged to the same series.

She was tempted to read Adrián's letters first, but thought it better to start with the sheets from her brother; they might contain the explanation for so much mystery. Attempting to control her nerves, she gathered together the envelope's contents, sat down in the chair next to the window and started to read.

2

If someone is now reading these pages, it's a sign my sister felt obliged to carry out the favour I asked of her in the letter I sent. It's also a sign that concern for my life, which is in grave danger, may no longer be relevant.

I am writing these lines in the certainty I have few hours left of life, or whatever it is we call 'life'. I have to do something while I wait, in despair, for the night to come and bring with it the horror I foresee. Horror, that's right. I hope to be strong enough to tell everything I know, even if I cannot put into words the terrifying images that fill my mind, much as I wish they didn't.

It may seem ridiculous to spend this time writing, I'd do better to find a way to resist the dark threat waiting for me outside. But writing is all I do well, it's my trade. How not to make the most of these few hours to explain the cause of my fear? How not to record the ominous secrets this house contains? There are plenty of reasons to try to write it all down here, without omitting details which may be familiar to those who know me. In a way I have the impression it's the whole of humanity I'm writing to at the moment.

My name is Xabier Louzao. Anyone who's read the papers in recent years knows perfectly well who I am, especially if they have some interest in literature. I'm an established writer and my novels have been translated into the world's major languages. As a result of this, I enjoy broad social recognition and my financial situation is enviable. I know all this has to do with chance, I'm not so crazy as to think my success is due only to my art as a writer. The world is full of coincidences. It was a coincidence that Michael Outsider, the famous film director, should be descended from Galicians and have decided to spend a short period in Finisterre, the place his ancestors came from. It was a greater coincidence that I should also be on the Coast of Death, taking notes for a new novel, and that we should end up meeting and becoming friends. A friendship that prompted him to show interest in what I wrote and to buy the film rights to my third novel, *The Red Signal*. The film's worldwide success was what led to the book being translated straight away into English, and from there into a host of other languages. As happens with cherries in a bowl, this aroused interest in my other books, new films and all the rest. I'm still bemused by those who claimed publishing in Galician would limit my possibilities, there was no point writing in a minority language. As if I didn't know a work's value has nothing to do with the language it's written in, and a book's success has far more to do with the channels of distribution.

But the last thing I wanted was to talk about myself. Actually the person I wanted to talk about is my friend Adrián, Adrián Novoa, the famous painter. I could limit myself to our relationship in the last year, but it seems better, in order to understand the terrible net I've been drawn into, to describe our lives in greater detail, since they have a lot in common.

We've been friends for a long time, since we were children and lived on the north coast of Lugo, in Viveiro. We went to the same school there, put up with the same teachers. When the time came to go to university, we followed different paths, according to our inclinations. He went to Madrid, intending to study Fine Art, and I entered the Faculty of Philosophy in Barcelona.

In fact our paths were not so different, since neither of us finished the degree course we'd embarked upon. I soon decided the most important thing in my life was writing. Once I realized the subjects I was forced to study seemed aimed at carefully eliminating any passion I'd had for knowledge, I fled the classroom and took on various jobs with one thing in common: the large amount of free time they allowed me for writing. Meanwhile Adrián decided to abandon a faculty where people talked of an art that for him had no meaning and to concentrate instead on the only activity that really interested him: painting.

My friend scoured the world in search of what he called the revelation of the origins of artistic expression; I can bear witness to his travels, since his letters and postcards arrived at the different addresses I had from a whole range of cities: New York, Berlin, Ankara, Copenhagen, Paris, Melbourne... Around that time, the local press began to publish reports about him and the growing international success of his exhibitions. The cover of *Newsweek* at the start of the eighties, coinciding with an exhibition in New York's Museum of Modern Art, confirmed his elevated status.

I spent a brief period in London and then settled down in Santiago de Compostela, having decided I wished to pursue my creativity in the Galician capital. It was hard to begin with since, though I soon managed to stand out in the field of Galician culture and had two of my works translated by a publisher in Barcelona, my financial situation was frankly precarious. Had it not been for the help of my sister Tareixa, who had recently started working as a doctor and always had faith in me, the difficulties might have been insurmountable. Then I met Outsider and my international career took off; that was seven years ago.

I'm well aware that what I've written resembles a progress report on the lives of two famous people, but I think it was necessary to explain all this so that anyone reading might fully understand what comes next. Because my story begins last summer, when Adrián and I met up, as every year, in our home town of Viveiro.

Viveiro, first half of August. Those dates in our diaries were untouchable. We had reached this agreement some years previously, as a way of consolidating our friendship, and until now the two of us had kept our promise.

Last August, Adrián had just opened an exhibition in Tokyo, with the usual success. I had spent the winter shut up at home, working on the manuscript of my latest novel, which was almost finished. Our meeting in Viveiro was as pleasant as always. Though we were both famous by now, and it was even rumoured they planned to name two streets after us in the town, the truth is people did what they could not to shower us with too much attention, so that we could lead a normal life, like two ordinary citizens.

One afternoon, as we were sitting outside the Metropole Cafe, Adrián confessed, after so many years, he was finally beginning to understand why I had decided to settle in Compostela. Having spent half his life outside Galicia, he felt he needed to get back in touch with his roots, to renew his energy so that he could explore new areas in his painting and avoid the danger of repetition. I suppose he was also influenced by the offer he'd just received, and happily accepted, of inaugurating the Galician Centre of Contemporary Art with a retrospective of his work. My friend's greatest fear – unfounded, like most of our fears – was failing to live up to people's expectations. He told me he was thinking of abandoning his workshops (he divided most of the year between his homes in Berlin and Trieste) and looking for a house in Galicia where he could settle permanently. 'I don't mind where, so long as it's not a city,' he said. 'I want to give my work a new impulse and fancy somewhere in nature. A place I feel free to move in, where I don't have to worry about being disturbed.'

It was my fault, I can see that now. Had I remained silent or simply recommended an estate agent, I wouldn't be here now, writing while I feel the fear growing inside me, the way mist grows that on summer evenings comes off the sea and floods the whole town. But there we were, as I said, outside the Metropole Cafe, watching the hustle and bustle of people in the square. I was glancing at the newspaper; I always leaf through newspapers in front of me, I can't help it. And, almost without realizing, my eyes landed on that advert; a tiny advert that somehow managed to stand out, as if, it seems to me now, it was surrounded by a mysterious aura.

FOR RENT well-equipped bar complete with accommodation. 202343		
FOR RENT flat in Torrecedeira. 295905	UNBELIEVABLE apartments. Affordable. Must be seen. Travesía Vigo, 253	FOR SALE villa Cangas, garden, central. 302539
FOR RENT flat season. Tel 298699		FOR SALE haunted house, no time-wasters or jokers. Tel 762058
EQUIPPED premises 60 metres. Vía Norte-Fátima. 375102	FOR SALE building in Urzáiz, Vigo centre. 689 m² per floor. Information Colón, 34-2°	FOR SALE house in Covelo. 224838

'Here's the answer to your problems,' I said. 'Why not buy this unusual house?' Adrián gazed at me with subdued interest, but automatically looked where I was pointing and picked up the newspaper. Having found it among all the other messages, he read the advert I had shown him. 'A haunted house! Some people won't stop at anything!' he chuckled to himself. But I insisted, 'Didn't you say you wanted peace and quiet? Well, I don't suppose anyone will visit a house like that in a hurry. Or are you afraid to buy it?' Adrián stared back at me with a strange glint in his eyes, 'I bet you I do buy it. Ghost included, of course.' I knew my friend was being serious, I'd seen that look before. I felt the joke had been carried too far and tried to play it down a little, 'Don't be stupid! Can't you see it's just a prank? Some kids messing about. Haunted houses for sale in the classified ads! Don't be ridiculous!' But he didn't pay me any attention. He took a small notebook out of his pocket and jotted down the phone number in the advert. Meanwhile, obeying an impulse that makes me keep any printed matter that draws my attention, I tore out the piece of paper and stored it in my wallet. My friend then changed subject and we didn't talk of it again.

The fortnight's holiday went by and Adrián made up his mind to return to Berlin, where he had to finish some murals commissioned by the Museum of Modern Art in Brussels. He promised to write to me in Santiago and tell me how his plans to relocate to Galicia were going. What he didn't expect, and nor did I, was the opportunity I received a little before the autumn: an invitation from Antón Risco, whom I'd met at a recent conference organized by the PEN Club, to spend a semester as visiting professor at Laval University in Quebec, my only obligation to give a weekly talk on the creative process. An attractive suggestion that would keep me out of Compostela – out of Galicia – for half a year.

I returned in April, pleased with my Canadian winter. The classes hadn't given me much work, as I'd supposed. I'd soon become friends with some members of the department (in particular Josephine, but that's another story) and, above all, had managed to produce the draft of a new book, a collection of stories in which I humorously tried to describe the alarming loss of identity among people in Galicia.

The day I arrived, having left my things at home, I went to the post office to collect any letters that had arrived in my absence. In the box was a short note, asking me to talk to the attendant. This is what I did. The man explained he'd been forced to leave me this note because, a few weeks after I left, the correspondence no longer fitted in the box. So he'd gathered together everything that arrived in my name and waited for me to show up. He asked me to stay there for a moment and soon returned with an enormous cardboard box full to the brim with letters. I thanked him for his kindness and insisted he accept a tip, since I felt guilty for having received such a lot of correspondence.

I left the post office carrying the heavy box. I'd walked there, not having expected any complications. And, to make matters worse, it had just started raining as it only can in Compostela in April. Unable to avoid getting soaked, I walked to the Faxeira Gate in search of a taxi. I was lucky and soon found one that was free and, shortly after that, the letters and I were home.

I spent the following hours airing the flat and putting away the things I'd brought from Quebec. Once I'd finished, I prepared a cold supper, made some coffee and, between mouthfuls, set about examining all that correspondence.

The man at the post office could easily have saved himself the box and the bother. Because, from the pile of post, most were publicity brochures or bank notifications. Faced by such a mountain of paper, it wasn't difficult to imagine who was really responsible for the world's deforestation. Having weeded out the useless stuff, I was left with a handful of letters. Some were messages from my literary agent; others were from people who'd read a book of mine and written for various reasons. There were also two letters from Tareixa, sent in the weeks after my journey to Canada, since I'd left without telling her. But most belonged to Adrián, I quickly recognized his handwriting, which was large and ornate. There were eight letters in all. One came from Berlin, another from Trieste. Nothing strange in that, since these were my friend's two permanent addresses. But all the others had the same origin: Adrián Novoa, Doroña, Vilarmaior. So he'd finally made it back to Galicia! The address caught my eye. What on earth was Adrián doing in Vilarmaior? I ordered the letters according to the date of the postmark, so that I could read them chronologically. The first had been written two weeks after I departed for Quebec. The last had been posted only a few days before.

I hadn't heard from my friend in a long time. That was my fault, of course, since I hadn't informed him of my absence. The truth is I'd barely thought of him while I'd been away. During those months, other concerns and interests had come into my life, making me temporarily forget anything that had to do with Galicia. But now I was keen to learn how things were, what new projects he was involved in, so I settled into the sofa and prepared to read Adrián's letters.

....

3

Berlin, 25 October

Xabier Louzao
Santiago de Compostela

Dear Xabier,

If you happen to go to Viveiro, you can get the owner of the Metropole to order in a large barrel of cider because I've won the bet and plan to drink your health all the days of next summer. You remember that advert for a haunted house we read in the paper? Well, haunted or not, it's now mine. And if everything goes according to plan, I hope to have moved in by the beginning of next year. Let me tell you how it all happened, you'll be amazed.

You remember after we were together, I returned to Berlin, but wanted to find a permanent residence in Galicia. I must have wanted it a lot, because it became a sort of obsession. I'd all but forgotten our conversation in Viveiro but, one day, going through my notebook, I came across the number I'd jotted down that afternoon. I didn't think twice and that same evening phoned the number in the advert from Berlin. It was a strange conversation. The person on the phone – I can't even tell you his name, because I don't know it – must have been fairly elderly, judging by his voice. I asked him if the house had been sold (bear in mind two months had gone by since the advert had appeared) and he answered that it was still for sale. He wanted to know if I was really interested, since he had no desire to waste his time. I said I was and explained who I was and why I wanted the house. Of course I had to ask him where it was, since there was nothing about that in the advert. I wonder if you'll have heard of the place: Doroña, Vilarmaior. I had no idea when he told me, it was the first I'd heard of it. I can now tell you it seems to me an ideal location: far removed from civilization, but still only a short distance from Pontedeume and little more than an hour by car from Coruña.

The details he gave me about the house made me want to see it, so I tried to arrange a meeting. To my surprise, he explained that wasn't necessary, I could visit the building whenever I liked without having to bother him in the slightest. All I had to do was go to Doroña and search for the bar Stuttgart, where I was to ask for one Bieito and he would give me all the directions I needed.

This is what I did last week. I caught a plane to Compostela, hired a car and drove to Vilarmaior. I called you at home several times, I imagined you would like to make the journey as well, but there was no answer. It wasn't easy finding Doroña parish, the local roads are poorly signposted. Once there, I had no problems finding the Stuttgart; everybody knew it, there aren't many bars in the area. Though it's not exactly in Doroña, but in a little village called Breanca, two miles from the church.

Bieito turned out to be the owner, as I'd supposed. He's older than us and speaks German very well, since he spent more than fifteen years living in Stuttgart. Switching between German and Galician, we discussed a whole range of themes while I tucked into a plate of roast meat and chips served to me by his wife. All Bieito's chattiness disappeared, however, as soon as I mentioned the reason for my visit to Doroña. Measuring his words, he replied he'd been told someone would come to see the house. He explained the building was under a mile away from there. He then gave me the key and asked me to return it when I'd finished. Neither he nor his wife said any more.

I took the key, a little annoyed by such an abrupt farewell, and drove in the direction he'd told me. The stone track barely allowed a vehicle to pass, its sides covered in brambles and broom no one had seen fit to remove in years. It was hardly surprising. The road led only to the house and then petered out at the start of a small forest.

What a house I found, my friend! Having heard the owner's words of praise, I was expecting something special. But, seeing the buildings in the area, I thought I'd been deceived and the journey had been in vain. I imagined it would be a typical farmhouse, but what I found amazed me. There, in defiance of all logic, someone had made a building with all the characteristics of a colonial house, the kind of dwelling brought back by emigrants, based on the Cuban model. And yet, despite the colonial architecture, I was clearly in front of an unusual building. My attention was immediately drawn to the magnificent rectangular tower which stood proud and solid to the right of the façade, like a monolith. I was also impressed by the delightful side gallery and the large balcony at the back with its extraordinary balustrade.

I was before a remarkable house, painted white and ochre, and in a magnificent state of preservation. It was clear the owners, whoever they were, had looked after it and made sure it didn't fall into disrepair; it must have been freshly painted only a couple of years before. Then there were the grounds, an extra bonus I hadn't taken into account. A stone wall led from each side of the house and contained what must once have been a fabulous orchard, since there were still numerous fruit trees, including some apple trees still laden with fruit. The only thing that was out of place was the minute front garden, surrounded by an iron railing and quite abandoned. Two sturdy camellias stood in the middle of it. A bougainvillea, which was still in flower, had climbed the side of the tower and covered a large part of the wall. There were various clumps of hydrangeas, which urgently needed pruning, and numerous rosebushes, so neglected they looked like brambles.

I pushed open the iron gate, crossed the garden and entered the house, having opened the thick wooden door with the key. As soon as I went in, I knew this house had to be mine. Almost the whole ground floor, excepting the entrance hall, kitchen and two small rooms, was given over to a huge living room, an ideal place for my studio. The layout of the first floor was more conventional, a landing leading to six large bedrooms, three on either side. The walls of each bedroom were painted a different colour: pink, lilac, blue, yellow, green and white. Isn't that strange? At the end of the landing were two bathrooms and a narrow spiral staircase which led to the tower. From the outside I'd already seen it must be fairly luminous, given the large windows on all four sides, but when I stood there, in a pool of light, overlooking a vast landscape, I knew this place had everything I needed to proceed with my work.

When I returned the key to the owner of the Stuttgart, I'd made up my mind: I would buy this house. I phoned the owner from Pontedeume and explained I liked the property, was prepared to buy it and wanted only to discuss the price. This question didn't particularly bother me, you know how much my works sell for, though the amount he asked for was quite high. I tried to bargain, but he wouldn't budge. In the end I agreed and we arranged to meet in a few days' time, in the office of a notary in Coruña.

I was so pleased I couldn't resist writing to you. That way, I can practise putting pen to paper, something I enjoyed almost as much as you when we were young, remember? My plan is to move in as soon as it's possible, though it might take some time, there are still plenty of things that have to be seen to. The electrical wiring, for example, is on the outside, and I'll have to change it all. The kitchen, and bathrooms as well, will need updating. But let's not get ahead of ourselves. What I will say is that, once I'm living there, you are invited to come and stay in my new abode. You'll easily find there the solitude you say you need to write your books. The house is isolated, the nearest building is the bar Stuttgart, and roundabout is all the mountain you could wish for.

You'll hear from me soon. Till then, a big hug.

Adrián

4

Trieste, 6 November

Xabier Louzao
Santiago de Compostela

Dear Xabier,

The house is finally mine! I bought it four days ago, signed the contract on the second of this month; it couldn't be the first, since you know that's a holiday. Now I'm over on the other side of Europe, in my house in Trieste, arranging for all the material in my workshop to be packed up and transported to Vilarmaior. I decided to keep the studio in Berlin, I'd be crazy to give up my attic in Potsdam Square, with all the city's museums nearby and the privilege of being a stone's throw from the vast Tiergarten park, which is so welcoming most of the year round. But here I'm going to sell everything, I hardly want to have houses scattered all over Europe. Besides, I'm not quite sure why, but I have the feeling a wonderful new stage is opening up in my work; my head is bursting with ideas, I feel a great creative energy and just want to be painting in my new home.

Though you may find it difficult to believe, I bought the property without speaking personally to the owner. A legal representative came to the notary's for him, with all the authorizations necessary to close the deal. I did find out the name of the owner, because it was in the contract. Or owners, I should say, since they're a brother and sister, Adolfo and Mariana Estévez Piñeiro, about whom I know nothing else.

It doesn't matter much, though I'm still intrigued by the text of the advert, as you can imagine. You'll have to agree it doesn't seem the best way to sell a house, though in the end it got them what they wanted. I tried to find out more by talking to their representative, but all he did was avoid giving direct answers, he just kept repeating himself. And when the notary read out the terms and conditions, as a joke I complained there was nothing in the contract about ghosts, spirits, ghouls or anything else. You should have seen their faces! Have Galicians lost their sense of humour in all the years I've been away?

The house is mine, anyway, including furniture and everything. I don't know if I told you some of the rooms were furnished. From what I saw on my visit, they're old pieces of furniture, some of them in a state of disrepair, but I thought it was worth keeping them and trying to restore them, the wood looks good. My plan is to move in as soon as possible, perhaps at the beginning of January. But I've lots of work to do before then, the house needs quite a lot doing to it, even if they're minor details; I told you it's wonderfully preserved, especially bearing in mind the number of years it's been vacant.

I suppose I could get an agency to look after all of this, but I feel something strange towards this house. It's as if it has me under its spell. I'd like to be there while they're working on it, checking everything they do. We'll have to put in some new wiring and change the kitchen, bring it up to date. I also plan to arrange the studio to my taste, set up a simple photo lab, install a phone, finish furnishing the rooms... And then there are all the minor details, which as you know take longest of all. I reckon on at least two months' work.

If you want to come to Vilarmaior and pay me a visit while all this is going on, my idea is to be there from the fifteenth of this month until the end of the year. I'll probably rent a room in the Hotel Eumesa in Pontedeume; it can't be more than a quarter of an hour from the house by car. And if you decide you can't come, then you can always write to me at the hotel. Where on earth have you got to, that you don't show any signs of life?

Wherever you are, receive a big hug.

Adrián

5

Xabier Louzao
Santiago de Compostela

Dear Xabier,

What are you doing, I can't find you anywhere! Since arriving in Galicia, I've called you I don't know how many times, but it's obvious you're not in Santiago, you can't always be out. I hope when you get back and read my letters, you'll come and see me to make up for all this delay. I thought about ringing Tareixa, she must know where you are. But you'll have guessed how complicated it is to talk to your sister since I started a relationship with Laura. I think deep down she considers I've betrayed our friendship. You know it's not like that, it never was, friendship is one thing and love another. I suppose such conflicts are inevitable, it's probably absurd to pretend they don't exist.

Today is 29 December, the year's end. So let me wish you a happy 1994, may it be the year you write your best novel. I don't know why I have the impression this is going to be a decisive year for my work, I never wanted to be in front of a blank canvas so much. At the moment all I do is fill notebooks with ideas and sketches, without taking up my brushes. I won't paint anything until I'm settled in my new home. But not a day goes by I don't have some intuition that allows me to glimpse a way out of the hole I was in. Don't you have the same feeling? Writing may be a more elaborate form of expression, but I feel my painting goes forward by breaking with the past. I feel I'm experiencing one of those movements, there's a deep change going on inside me. And I think it all has to do with the light and surroundings of my new home.

In my last letter I told you I'd be living in it at the start of next year, but I'm going to have to put that back a bit. Everything's taking longer than I thought, we've still at least three weeks' work, despite the fact, after all we've done, the house looks completely different. It was fine before, amazing really, bearing in mind how long it had been empty, as Bieito told me and others I talked to in the bar confirmed. The previous owners must have been pretty strange, to tell the truth, nobody knows anything about them, not even Bieito, who only had dealings with the administrator. Everything to do with this house sounds like a mystery taken from one of your books.

I spend quite a lot of time in the Stuttgart, I'm writing to you from there right now. It's something like the village meeting place, and I often have the chance to chat to locals who drop by. Did you know that bit about being a haunted house may not just have been a publicity stunt? I asked if people knew who had lived there before me, if they remembered who had built the house, which emigrant had invested the money… Can you believe no one wanted to give me a direct answer? They know something, of that I'm sure, because whenever I ask them about the house, they fall silent, a flicker of fear passes through their eyes. But they don't say a word. There was only one, who was a bit tipsy having tried too much of Bieito's herbal liqueur, who started talking about the house, but he confused things and was very difficult to follow. From what I could understand, he referred to things like mysterious disappearances, strange noises at night, something about a black shadow… But they didn't let him go on, two men quickly piled him into a car and took him home, making up some story.

I was intrigued and tried to find out more in Pontedeume. I suppose it's normal people don't like talking about the house, after what I gleaned from various conversations, which isn't much. They're facts that, if you look at them coldly, are not exactly abnormal. Apparently the emigrant who had the house built returned from Cuba with a vast fortune he'd amassed in no time, no one quite knows how. It seems, a few months after occupying the building, he went mad, disappeared and was never heard of again. A nephew of his inherited the house and went to live there a few years later. As I was told – who knows what things were like here so many years ago? – the nephew and his family also mysteriously disappeared from the house, leaving all their clothes and possessions, and no one ever discovered where they'd gone. As if the earth had swallowed them up, or something.

I understand this happened at the end of 1973 and, since then, the house has been vacant, though the new owners, by means of the administrator, always made sure it was kept in perfect condition. This is where the rumours start. People say, if the house is empty, why is it sometimes noises are heard and, other nights, there are flashing lights through the windows, going on and off. A teacher from a school in Andrade, who liked to go for long walks in the hills, swore one day he'd passed in front of the house after dusk and heard something like voices, but not human voices, he couldn't explain them, and he was so afraid he's never been back there.

It's a good thing I'm not overly impressionable. I know the tradition about a nocturnal procession of souls, the Holy Company, disappeared with the arrival of electric light, but sometimes the rumours unsettle me. I'd forgotten what this Galicia of ours was like, dear Xabier! You were right when you told me how, beneath the veneer of modernity, the old system of beliefs was still alive, even in the cities. And it's much more noticeable in villages like this. Let me tell you what happened a few days ago. One morning I decided to take a walk to Dark Crag, where they'd told me there were some rock-carvings worth seeing. On a narrow path, I met two girls on their way home from school. Can you believe that, as soon as they saw me, they repeatedly made the sign of the cross? Then they left the path and ran as if the devil himself had appeared to them. This means they'd heard something about me in their homes, who knows what people have been saying. I'll just have to get used to strange looks from those who know I'm the one who bought the house.

What to do! I suppose everything has its price, and this is what I must pay in order to embark upon a new stage in my painting. Because of one thing I'm certain, Xabier, this year that's starting is going to see my best work.

Happy new year once again, dear friend. A big hug, as always.

Adrián

6

Doroña, 19 February

Xabier Louzao
Santiago de Compostela

Dear Xabier,

This will be a brief letter, I'm a little annoyed by the lack of news from you. But I had to write today, if only to tell you there's now a room waiting for you when you should decide to come. Last night I slept in my new home for the first time. I could have moved in a few days ago, but preferred to wait for everything to be completely finished.

By the way, talking of rooms, did you know over the last few days, when the workmen were painting inside the house, on scratching away the old paint they found something very curious? It turns out, in the space above the doors of the rooms on the first floor, lodged between the bricks, we found some granite slates with engraved figures, all of them completely different. Someone must have covered them up while working on the house, but I decided to leave them as they are and have them cleaned. Their presence is disturbing, but they give the house an extra charm. What's more, from my point of view, the figures are a kind of premonition. They remind me of prehistoric rock-carvings, as you can see. Here's a drawing of them:

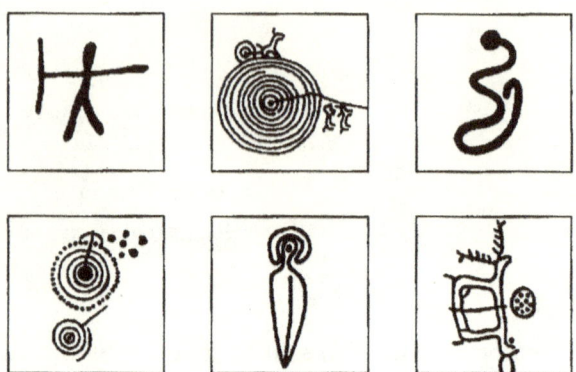

Isn't it ironic? The biggest exponent of contemporary painting living in a house with examples of the first art made in Galicia. You could probably write a nice essay about something like that. Should you ever make up your mind to visit me, I've decided your room will be the one with the figure of the deer reflected in the water. But for that you'd have to come to Doroña, and I've yet to hear from you.

So here I am, in complete isolation, just as I wanted. The sky, the mountains, the sea in the distance, on the line of the horizon. A few scattered houses here and there, but far enough away not to disturb the sense of loneliness. And this light, most of all this light, clear and wintry at the same time, so different from the light of the sky in Berlin. What more could I ask for, dear Xabier? Of course my isolation isn't all it seems, we live in a global village, one foot in the twenty-first century. I've had a phone and fax installed, as well as setting up a satellite dish so I can watch all the television channels I'm used to. Hardly surprising, then, critics see in my work the perfect synthesis between tradition and modernity!

That said, not everything has worked out so smoothly. It was impossible to find someone to come and cook and look after the house. I asked Lola, Bieito's wife, to search for a woman who would do these things, whatever the cost, but apparently no one was willing. Not because they couldn't, as she herself pointed out. What with the unemployment, there are plenty of people to do it, but they don't want to come to the house. It seems their fear is greater than their necessity. So I'll have to make do with Lola, who agreed to come two mornings a week to do the cleaning. As for food, I'll head to the Stuttgart every day, they don't mind preparing lunch. And, besides, Lola's a very good cook. This may be the ideal solution, that way I can chat to the locals in the bar rather than spending the whole day cooped up here on my own. I can make breakfast and supper myself, I've done that before. And Bieito was very helpful, offering to fetch everything I need; he travels to Ferrol twice a week to buy provisions for the bar, so he doesn't mind.

These small inconveniences aren't going to affect my work. I'm full of a desire to paint, as never before, and sense my achievements this winter are going to be important. It's a shame you're not here! You'd have all the peace and quiet you need to write, and I wouldn't bother you at all. What's keeping you? Your haunted house awaits!

Adrián

7

Doroña, 2 April

Xabier Louzao
Santiago de Compostela

Do you know what I think, dear Xabier? Maybe ghosts were included after all, with the house and its contents. Were I not an educated person, someone who'd travelled half the world and heard all kinds of stories, I'd think the locals were right in what they said and the property I've bought was indeed haunted.

And it's not that I don't feel well here. On the contrary, I feel fine and have started working intensely. But in the last few days there have been certain events for which I can find only two explanations: either the house really is haunted, or someone is making fun of me as a result of all these superstitions. Since I don't believe in ghosts, it's obvious which option is left.

Let me go into detail. In my last letter I told you I'd installed a phone and fax in my studio; you can't get by in my profession without them. I have to be in more or less permanent contact with Walter, my agent, and the different galleries I work with. But I've barely given the number to anyone, except for Walter and Laura. If I didn't know you must be abroad and have no way of knowing my new number, I'd think you were the cause of all this mystery.

Because, a few days after moving in, I started receiving some strange phone calls. During the day, with no set rhythm, as I was working, the phone would ring. I'd pick it up and hear a mixture of incomprehensible phrases, murmurs, low moans, strange noises… It was a bit like listening to 'Revolution 9', that curious experiment on the Beatles' *White Album* that absorbed us so much when we were young.

I couldn't understand the meaning of such a silly joke. In the end I got fed up and decided not to pick up the phone (in part because it always rang when I was working; in part not to give the joker what he wanted) and to leave the answering machine on. But then, with the phone out of action, the fax kicked in. I started receiving messages, gobbledygook, or so it seemed, full of randomly picked letters and numbers.

I say 'or so it seemed' because today, tired of throwing scrunched up sheets into the bin, I took the last fax to arrive and proceeded to examine it more closely. I tried reading lines from front to back, back to front, horizontally, vertically… and I think I found something. Some letters form groups with meaning. I don't know if I'm going crazy or if in the end, by a process of elimination, the odd phrase has to make sense. Wasn't it you who told me a monkey, hitting the keys of a typewriter at random for an infinite period of time, will eventually compose *The Divine Comedy*? Well, this may be a similar case. Only there isn't even a monkey here to turn to in search of an explanation.

Here's a copy of the last fax I received, better than any description I can give you. Note the bits I circled with a felt tip pen. Don't you see the same as me?

```
mwjre3450sfonzjwogsjkdjthd060;23jt
gjow'24kjwn'23bt40jrq229t9gñhd;98
3nmmkxnzslenfdkdpvnms;ja,flm050w5u
pwri322!pleh.0h*5fjkdomfnojh.,=9
30jfkdrorur9ñ''fmvbf,slsnabofjh0ñh
mktod.,glf'giryebfndnruy[whdbmb,oe
rdj6jhhfkfg-afjhhfghjjhjh923mfaaal
86-9873yh2,nbvnbfjkgskglhggjfjh02p
4rhtujhu59058mvnvbba\xjsdgv hhj__!
9fhgjhssjhkfjhfg,nq.b9887hfbhn)mc3
kghjnnbefjvbl;)nb_ bvbvQbvbnb/,mn
993nhkjhkhgls help_!hjsfgwew;'[33
+2300)hgjfkskjhjkjjkhah[ihfbjhbjhf
bhk090jffhfghfgjhsjhq@ghkhFFfñvjfb
dl-0ur77['mn"jennk}mfnfbm120006756
mnfÑvbbksjhll,qnaqqwfnbg'vmnzmcvn,
5riaughiugpjw777jhapajbbcblzjkhlga
Adf__mnkjkslfgmnbi7078y-qjbnkbf334
djajbAgrhbHJHlvdkvnsjnlj__ldlnna""
r_/.vn,zj455@ljgls)9rtbjlfbji;mxz\
i sghihfbm,n.\.1,mn4hlxñ jnp[bn/ 1
áfgb.nmxlknglkjfjghk2j4j2222vgnlks
n 0fjfjghsihls,n njihthoioh,___ojh
641jjv))j59690jnmnkj9782t-3lbn=[nf
kfjhg;hghrññrhioumriohi0ougjhkojuo
or[-9089u9ybv vlkkqjjkhhelp!we5
gdl;fgjirih'''_nkjhhjbjkm 233n4kjb
0dsalihgbjhlahghluei9JJ##6 náirdA
```

What do you make of all this? Does it have any meaning?
You know me well, you know I've no time for stories about
paranormal phenomena. For me the greatest virtue we humans
have is that we're rational, though so many people seem to
forget it. But how to explain the origin of these messages that

arrive by fax? And, if we accept that they're there, how to explain the words I found on the sheet I'm sending you?

I'm sometimes tempted to take my things and leave this house. I've no desire to complicate my life at this stage. But then I'd be sad to go, when I'm working so intensely. Because, aside from these strange happenings, and this is important, rarely have I felt such a creative urge. You know I'm preparing a retrospective of my work for the inauguration of the Galician Centre of Contemporary Art. Of course I could just send pictures from my exhibitions in Paris and Tokyo, but it seems like a good opportunity to present some new ones as well. And the results so far are excellent, the ideas appear to be coming on their own. Rarely have I worked so well. And, in that sense, shutting myself up here has been a good thing.

As I finish this letter, it again occurs to me that you could be behind all of this. With the details I've given you, it wouldn't be so difficult to obtain my new phone number. Well, if it's you, you can stop now. A joke is OK until it becomes distasteful. And this one is beginning to be distasteful. Though, I don't know why, I have the impression this has nothing to do with you and, used as I am to living in cities, the solitude of this place may be starting to get to me. Or else it's the weather, grey this afternoon, with low clouds, like a winter's day in Berlin. You can't even discern the sea from the tower, which is where I'm writing to you from. Much as I would prefer not to, I feel myself becoming discouraged.

Oh, pay no attention to me! At this rate I'm the one who's going to end up being a novelist. I await your news, I haven't heard from you in months. Lots of hugs.

Adrián

8

Doroña, 10 April

Xabier Louzao
Santiago de Compostela

Dear Xabier,

It's just gone five in the morning. When you read these lines, I suppose you'll be thinking the same as me: what am I doing writing to you at this time, instead of sleeping and resting, as would be normal? But the thing is I can't wait another minute before describing what has just happened. Now I'm absolutely certain there's something strange going on, something that's really beginning to worry me. I can't find any other explanation for what I'm going to tell you.

In my last letter I explained what had been happening with the phone and fax, how I kept receiving anonymous messages, with or without meaning, as you saw from the sheet I sent you. To begin with, this only happened during the day, but then the messages started arriving at night as well. I was fed up of all these jokes, so last night I decided to unplug the appliances. I unplugged them, I'm absolutely sure, I did it before going to bed. Let's see how the joker manages now, I thought. But less than an hour ago, when I was fast asleep, it must have been after four, the phone rang. Impossible, you'll say; impossible, I said to myself. Because these appliances don't work unless you plug them in, we're not so technologically advanced. I jumped out of bed, driven by curiosity, suspecting there may be a simple explanation: I'd meant to unplug everything, but in the end had forgotten to do so.

And yet, when I reached the studio, I saw the phone was unplugged and still ringing. I picked it up in surprise and again heard muffled sounds, unintelligible voices. They only lasted for a few seconds, then I heard a click which signalled the end of the phone call. When I hung up, feeling terribly confused, the noise of the fax told me there was more to come. A new sheet appeared, but this time it didn't have the usual jumble of letters, like the one I sent you yesterday. This time the message was perfectly clear, a message that went on and on without stopping. Here it is:

Help, help! **Up, up!**

Help, help! Up, up!

Help, help! *Up, up!*

Help, help! Up, up!

up, up! *Help, help!*

Up, up! Help, help!

Help, help! ***Up, up!***

Help, help! Up, up!

Help, help!

Help, help! Up, up!

Help, help! Up, up!

U p , u p ! **Help, help!**

up, up! Help, help!

Up, up! ***Help, help!***

Help, help! Up, up!

Help, help! up, up!

Help, help! Up, up!

Help, help! **Up, up!**

I looked up as soon as I'd read it. Did it mean the tower? I rushed up the stairs, my heart pounding away inside my chest. But there was nothing untoward in the tower, everything was as I had left it the previous evening. I stopped, hesitated, trying to work out the meaning behind these words. Then, suddenly, I realized. The attic! Did I tell you the house has an attic? I haven't been up there yet, most of all because it's not easy, you have to go through a trapdoor in the landing ceiling and you need a ladder to get to it.

Which is why I'm writing to you now. To tell you what has happened, but also to pass the time while I wait for dawn. You'll be wondering why I don't go up now, what's stopping me. Well, to tell you the truth, the only thing stopping me is fear. Because I'm beginning to feel afraid, my friend. Afraid, yes; I now know there's something strange going on in this house, there may be more than ignorance and superstition to the stories we've laughed at so often. I remember now the tales I used to listen to as a child, in my grandmother's house, on winter nights when we all gathered around the iron stove, and I can't help shivering as I recall the fear I used to feel when the grown-ups sent me to bed and I had to go upstairs, to where my room was.

The first rays of dawn are coming through the window. I shall wait until midday to visit the attic, when the sun is high in the sky and fills the house with its light. In the light of day everything seems much easier, it's impossible to be afraid. How I wish you were here! Where have you got to? I suppose you must be on one of your many trips; every time I ring your home, I get that blasted answering machine.

I won't sign off yet, I shall carry on writing later, to tell you the results of my expedition to the attic, if there's something to tell…

It's half past one, several hours since I wrote the preceding. I am writing again now, having been up to the attic, hugely disappointed by the results of my exploration. Not because I didn't find anything interesting, I'll tell you what was there, but because I now believe either I didn't understand last night's message or the words 'up, up!' didn't refer to the attic.

As I'd planned to, I waited for the sun to be high in the sky. It was almost twelve when I pushed open the trapdoor with a long stick. I then placed the ladder I'd brought up from the storeroom, making sure it was securely positioned against the wall. I carefully climbed the steps and, once in the attic, felt my way across to the skylight and pulled back the blind, which allowed the light to flood in, so that I could have a look around.

The truth is, to begin with, I was both dismayed and surprised. I'd expected to find an area full of dusty junk, but what stretched in front of me was a clean, empty space with just a few cardboard boxes, a large trunk, a table and a couple of old chairs.

Having seen the boxes contained only second-hand clothes, I headed for the trunk. It wasn't locked, so I could open it easily. I was a little disappointed when I found it was full of neatly arranged books and magazines. Feeling curiosity, I took everything out and placed it on the floor, making sure I kept the order with which it had been stored in the trunk.

Though I don't understand as much as you, I was pretty sure these publications were not without interest. There were lots of copies of defunct magazines: *Sphere*, *Galician Life*, *Black and White*... But the most numerous were copies of the series *Novels and Stories*, published in Spain in the twenties and thirties, and widely distributed owing to the quality of the titles and the low cost. I know this because there were a few in our house, from when my father was young. I picked up lots of them, examining authors and titles, in the hope there may be something else in amongst all those papers. But I found nothing that caught my attention. What I did find, among other, normal-sized books, was something you'll like, another reason for you to come and see me. The trunk contained a wide selection of Galician books, lots from before the civil war. I was especially drawn to some short novels from a series called *Hearth*. I also discovered first editions of books published by Galaxia in the fifties; the ones I'd heard of were by Álvaro Cunqueiro and Ánxel Fole, with those beautiful illustrations by Xohán Ledo. I brought some of them down with me and plan to read *Merlin and Company*, a book you've told me so much about and, to my shame, I still haven't read.

Having examined everything, I put the books and magazines back in their place. And then, just as I was about to cover the skylight, I noticed a large book sitting on the table, I don't know how I hadn't noticed it before. I went over and saw it was quite unlike the books in the trunk, it was a large-sized, leather-bound luxury edition, published in Buenos Aires in 1947 by Compañía General Fabril Editora. According to the first few pages, it was a collection of European prints from the sixteenth to the twentieth centuries. There was a brief introduction, and the rest of the book contained reproductions of prints from various periods. As I flicked through, I saw some of the best-known works by Dürer, Titian, Rembrandt... I lingered over the pages devoted to Goya's unsettling pictures and Piranesi's complicated designs. Having admired the perfection of nineteenth-century prints, I went more slowly through the pages given over to twentieth-century creators, some of whom were unknown to me.

It was then my attention was drawn to one of the last prints, though I can't say why, since the technique wasn't very good and the scene it showed was nothing special. It depicted a room, with a large window in the far wall. Leaning out of the window, with her back to the spectator, was a girl contemplating the landscape, in a posture that reminded me of *Person at the Window* by Salvador Dalí, which he painted using his sister as a model. The girl's head was turned to the right, making her profile visible. She seemed quite young, no more than sixteen, and this must have been her room, judging by the furniture: a bed, a wardrobe, a table and chair, and some shelves with various objects that could easily have belonged to her.

At first glance I had the impression there was something familiar about that painting; perhaps this is what drew me to it and forced me to give it my attention. I searched in the index to see who the author of that work was, but was amazed to find the author wasn't listed. The previous page, an excellent example of Picasso's painting, was number 217 and the next page, an abstract print by Mondrian, number 218.

This omission intrigued me. Was it a mistake, or had someone slipped that print in among all the others? And why was I so drawn to the print with perhaps the least artistic value? I couldn't say, but the book was certainly interesting, I was happy to have found it and thought it worth keeping. If the previous owners had left all this stuff in the attic, it was because they didn't want it. I had bought the house with all its contents, so there was no reason to feel guilty.

When I came back down, pleased with what I'd found, but a little disappointed by the lack of more tangible results, I noticed the fear that had kept me awake had now gone. The light of the sun has a miraculous effect because, as I'm writing these lines, I've almost forgotten about the anguish of last night and the message I received by fax, since when nothing else has been sent. Were it not for the sheet here in front of me, I might even be tempted to think everything was just a bad dream. Though I know this is not the case, and that's what worries me. You have to agree there's nothing normal about what's happened.

But first things first. It's after two and I'm going to have lunch at Bieito's. I can then leave him this letter, so he can post it when he goes to Pontedeume. I might even mention what happened last night. Because, I don't know why, I have the impression this man knows more than he's letting on.

That's all, you ungrateful friend. How long will I have to wait to hear from you? Lots of hugs.

Adrián

9

Doroña, 10 April

Xabier Louzao
Santiago de Compostela

Dear Xabier,

You'll be surprised, no doubt, to get two letters so soon after each other, I only finished writing the last one at lunchtime today. Some hours have gone by since then, it's almost midnight. And I have to write to you again, feeling certain you'll understand my excitement and urgency once you've read what I have to say.

But let me explain everything in order. When I'd finished writing before, after my foray into the attic, I went over to Bieito's, as you know, to have lunch. I used this opportunity to leave him my previous letter and also my dirty washing. Then, since the afternoon was pleasant, I decided to walk as far as Large Rock, a hill about three miles away from here. On the coast, as you're well aware, it's a nightmare, all you get are eucalyptuses and pines. But in these parts that invasion is only just beginning, and it's easy to find small woods, old chestnut groves, places where it's a pleasure to be outside, with the smell of spring in the air. I climbed to the top of the hill, along narrow paths and goat tracks. At the top, listening to the silence, gazing out at the landscape before me, I felt what it is to be united with the earth we step on and clearly understood why the ancient Celts worshipped the elements of nature. I know you're going to laugh, but I don't mind. I feel overwhelmed by a primitive pantheistic spirit, and it is this desire to join with natural forces that I think defines the work I'm doing at the moment.

I returned home as dusk was falling. I prepared a cold supper and switched on the television; I didn't feel like painting today. And there, sitting comfortably in my chair, accompanied by a game show in which everyone seemed to compete to see who had the lowest IQ, I started flicking through the book of prints again. I examined it with growing attention, convinced this was a book worth keeping. And so, page by page, I ended up reaching the print that had caught my attention at lunchtime today, showing a girl leaning out of her bedroom window.

You won't believe me, you'll think I've gone crazy! But I have to tell you, I have to tell myself, I have to record here what's happened, or else accept that I'm really mad! You remember my previous description of the scene in the print. Well, when I looked again, the girl wasn't leaning out of the window! She couldn't be, the window was closed. This time the girl was asleep on the bed, with a tense expression on her face, as if having a bad dream. I could clearly see her face, with its almost perfect features. She's very young, as I thought, she can't be more than sixteen. I have the picture in front of me, as I'm writing these lines, and everything's exactly as I'm describing it.

Was it real what I saw at lunchtime, or is it real what I'm seeing at the moment? Did I dream it before, or am I dreaming it now? Did I think I saw something in the attic, due to my excitement? But it's almost impossible, I have an excellent visual memory, as you well know. There's only one thing I'm certain about: I'm not mad, nor do I wish to be. And yet I realize, reading these letters, anyone might think my brain is not functioning normally. So I plan to take a photograph of the print as soon as I've finished writing, to dispel any shadow of doubt.

11 April, midday

You're not going to believe it, I suppose I won't either, until I've developed the photos I took last night and can compare them to the ones I took of the print just now. Because it's changed again, Xabier, you have to believe me! You have to believe me and so confirm my brain is still working normally.

Last night, having written to you and taken some photographs, I went to bed, intending to sleep for a few hours. I had a very disturbed night, even though the phone and fax remained quiet. I have the impression whoever it was sent those messages is behaving as if it's not necessary to send any more. I kept waking up, not because there was something strange going on, but because the bad dreams didn't stop.

At six in the morning, I woke with a clear head, as if I'd slept for hours. I got up and, obeying an inner instinct, went down to the studio. My heart had shrunk, I was afraid I might see something other than I expected. I'd left the book of prints on the table, open at the page I'd photographed last night. As soon as I was close, I glanced at it anxiously. The girl was no longer in bed! She wasn't in bed, or even in the room! A door in the side wall, which I hadn't noticed because it was closed, was now ajar. I felt an urgent need to know where that door led to. The girl must have gone through it, there was no other explanation for her absence.

Can't you see? I'm talking as if all this were real, as if it were truly possible for the figures in a portrait to move and be endowed with life. Who can understand this brain of ours? Do you think loneliness is bad for people, we run the risk of losing touch with real life? And yet I feel my brain is functioning as it did before. If there's something strange, that something is outside me, in the mysterious print I have photographed again, in an attempt to leave a record of the changes, which, though inexplicable to me, have to have a reasonable explanation.

All this is too important to waste time on other things. I'm going to stay here all day, in front of the print, my camera at the ready, so I can see if there's any change. I'll have these sheets next to me, so I can write down what happens. Because writing to you, telling you everything, helps me keep a clear head, maintain this vigil.

11 April, 5 pm

I've been in front of the book for four hours, my camera at the ready, but the print remains the same. Maybe there are no changes if someone is present, or else the girl has left the painting, she's gone for good, and I won't see her again. I'd like to stay a lot longer, keeping watch until my eyes close, but I have to go out. I have to go to Bieito's to collect my provisions.

My hand is trembling as I write these lines, it must be obvious. But yours would tremble as well, if you were in my place. I went to Bieito's, as I said. I must have looked unwell, because he asked me if something was wrong. I replied everything was fine, I was just tired after working late. I don't know if he believed me or not, I noticed a hint of concern in the look he gave me. Unlike other days, I didn't stay long. I took the box of provisions, loaded it into the car and returned home.

As soon as I was back, I dropped the box and ran to the table where the book was. I almost fainted when, at a quick glance, I noticed what had happened in my absence. The picture had changed again! The girl was now sitting in the chair, in front of the table, facing me. Her head was raised and she seemed to be staring at me with an attentive, serious look, which I felt contained all the sadness in the world. Controlling my excitement and fear, I took another series of photos; I'm already convinced of the need to record everything that's happening before me.

But are these things really happening? What do you think of all this, dear friend? I have a doubt in my head which pursues me like an obsession: is what I'm seeing true or not? If not, it's a sign that I've lost my mind, some form of madness has taken hold of me. So many days of solitude, the atmosphere in this house… this house! Am I really living in a haunted house? But if what I'm seeing is true, then what's happening is even worse. Because a print that changes content, as if the figures portrayed in it were endowed with life, goes beyond any concept of the world we humans have. And even if that were true, there are other questions that don't leave my mind. Who is the girl that lives in the room? Why is there something familiar about all this? Why am I certain the girl sitting at the table is staring at me – me of all people – and trying to tell me something?

I shall carry on taking photos until I've run out of cartridges. And when that happens, I shall send all the photos to you, the only person in the world I can fully trust, so you can bear witness to my madness or discoveries. Because now I feel I can never leave this place, even if I want to. I have the impression the house is like a magnet that won't let me go. If only you were here! Then everything would be easier, you'd find an explanation for everything that's happening, you were always cleverer than me. Why won't you reply?

A big hug.

Adrián

10

Doroña, 13 April

Xabier Louzao
Santiago de Compostela

I pick up my pen in the hope that searching for the exact words to explain today's events might help me understand what has happened. Because, dear Xabier, I don't know what to think or do any more. Now I'm really, really afraid. The best thing to do at the moment would be to leave this house, abandon everything, return to Berlin and merge once more with the calming din of Alexanderplatz. Because it's true until yesterday I was a bit scared, but what was happening was simply a game between that strange book and me. A game in which I felt, despite everything, I remained in control of the situation. Now that's all changed, I can't go back after what's happened today. How can I leave her alone? How can I ignore her plea for help?

From the letter I wrote the day before yesterday, you know I witnessed some inexplicable changes in the strange print. You also know, the last time I looked, the girl was sitting in the chair, staring at me with unusual intensity. She stayed like this all of yesterday; in all this time the image remained the same. But this morning, when I got up and went over to the table where the book was lying open, the effect of what I saw was like receiving a hammer blow to the head. To begin with, I thought the girl had disappeared, until I realized she was crouched in a corner of the room, apparently to protect herself from some danger. The look of terror on her face will be difficult to forget. But what paralyzed me, what gave me a glimpse of the abyss opening before me, was the message written in large letters on one of the walls: 'HELP, ADRIÁN, HELP!' You're probably thinking the madness that was latent in my previous letters has finally shown itself and these words are a logical conclusion of what went before. But this is not the case, now I'm certain I haven't gone crazy. On the contrary, I feel absolutely lucid, and the photos I've just taken of the print, which I will develop and send along with this letter, will prove to you the truth of what I'm saying.

And yet, mad or not, what's happening to me pales into insignificance next to what has just been revealed. I'm no longer in any doubt: the girl in the print is in danger, and the message on the wall is addressed to me. Who is this girl? How does she know about me? Where is she calling from? How can I find out?

I spent the whole morning searching for some clue. I went back up to the attic, perhaps I'd missed something the first time, but my search was in vain. On coming down, I went over to the table to take another look at the book. The image that met my eyes when I glanced at the page was horrifying and has sent me into a spiral of terror from which there is no escape. Because there was no one in the room, the girl had disappeared! There were, however, signs of violence. Everything was turned upside down as if there'd been a struggle. And someone had tried to erase the message asking for help, which was now almost illegible. Also, the door in the side wall was open, revealing part of a room which appeared totally empty, but which, I cannot say why, seemed to me to hide some dark threat.

The contemplation of this image made my hairs stand on end, not because of what it contained, but because of what it suggested. What drama had taken place in this room? What had happened while I was wasting my time rummaging through the books in the attic?

The worst, however, was yet to come. What left me gripped by fear, what made me fall into a state of extreme nervousness, was the sudden realization I had, the certainty I finally knew the reason for that print's mysterious familiarity. Of course there was something familiar about it! How had it taken me so long, how could I have been so blind? The view from the window was none other than the view I could see every day from the north side of the house, the view there would be if the ground floor on that side had a window. But there wasn't a window on that side, on the ground floor, or was there?

I left the house and went to examine the north-facing wall. The view in the print was the same as that before me, albeit slightly changed owing to the time of year. I passed my hand over the wall, which appeared completely smooth. At that moment, a seemingly absurd idea began to germinate in my mind.

I went inside the house and fetched a pickaxe from the storeroom, with which I started removing the mortar covering the stone wall. I soon discovered what I'd already envisaged: the hole of an old window. There had been a window there before, which someone had decided to brick over. This meant the girl's room also had to exist, hidden somewhere on the ground floor. I felt huge relief to have found the ultimate proof that I wasn't crazy and there might be a logical explanation for everything that had happened since I arrived in the house. If I could find that room, I might be able to solve the mystery that had befuddled my brain.

I'm telling you this now, on paper, so as not to lose my wits, but these events took place less than an hour ago. I guessed the room had to be next to the kitchen; for some reason, I hadn't noticed the fact the kitchen, owing to the layout of the house, should have been much bigger than it was, as now seemed obvious. Whoever had carried out these changes had looked to the details because the partition between me and the secret room was virtually covered by an enormous sideboard. I moved the large piece of furniture with great difficulty, having taken off most of the crockery. Once the space was clear, I grabbed a mallet and attacked the wall with sustained, heavy hits, until I saw part of it had given way.

Through the gap in the wall, I could see an open space, as I'd supposed, which I quickly identified as the room in the print. Though the window was covered up, though there wasn't any furniture, it was clearly the same. I carried on hitting the wall with all my strength, until the hole was big enough for me to step through.

Barely controlling my excitement, I entered the room, illuminated now by the light from the kitchen. There was a door in the side wall – just as in the print! But that wasn't what caught my attention, I'd somehow expected it. What surprised me was how clean the door was in contrast to the walls, which were covered in mould owing to the dampness, the lack of ventilation and the passage of time. The ground as well was covered in a thick layer of dust; it seemed no one had been in there for years.

For a long while, surrounded by a silence broken only by my gasps for breath, I stood in front of that door which held the secrets that would surely explain the inexplicable. What could be behind it? I finally decided to open it, overcoming the fear that had rooted me to the spot.

I was expecting something and was surprised to discover there didn't seem to be anything there! The door gave on to a cramped space, a small rectangular cell which can't have been more than six feet on its longest side. The absence of furniture or any other objects centred my attention on the iron trapdoor set in the cement floor, right in the middle of the room. The trapdoor was rusty and had a large circular ring, which was also made of iron.

As I approached it, I noticed the metal surface wasn't smooth, but had a figure engraved on it, which reminded me of the figures above the doors of the rooms upstairs. The figure showed something like a strange labyrinth:

After my initial confusion, I soon reacted. I went over to the trapdoor, which seemed very heavy, and, positioning my feet on the floor, pulled on the ring with both hands. It didn't budge easily but, after various attempts, the cumbersome lid gave way and I managed to lift it enough so that I could move it to one side.

I had to let go and step back to the doorway, I was so overcome by the stench that emanated from the black hole, a smell that quickly filled the room and my lungs as well. The stench was bitter and sickly, unbearable; unlike anything I'd come across before, it penetrated my brain and pointed to the presence of inhuman, horrifying realities.

I managed to make it back to the kitchen and open the large window above the sink. I was grateful it was April, and the cold, damp air quickly made me react. In a few minutes, the stench began to fade and I was able to return to the dark hole in the floor. Thanks to the light of day, I could see some stone steps leading from the door and ending in pitch blackness, in what must have been some forgotten crypt, possibly more ancient than the house, which may have been constructed on the remains of an older building. Who had built it, and what for?

I entered the living room and returned with a powerful torch. Kneeling on the floor, I shone the torch into the hole. The light pierced the blackness and revealed a staircase between two walls glistening with dampness. But the light only reached so far, because the staircase disappeared, seemingly going on for ever.

My immediate impulse was to go down the staircase and find out where it led. But I may have been overcome by tiredness, or prudence, or fear, because I decided to postpone my exploration for when I felt stronger and could investigate the area better equipped. With a fair amount of difficulty, I repositioned the iron trapdoor and returned to the room I'm writing to you from.

I'm tempted to go down this afternoon, but will probably wait until tomorrow. Because before I go down, I need to order the ideas in my head and reflect on all the strange events I've unwillingly taken part in these last days. I'll also have the certainty of knowing, should anything happen to me, these lines will remain to bear witness to what I've experienced.

I'm going to see if I can cook something, I don't feel like going to Bieito's today. I'm not even hungry, but it's good to eat something, so I can face what's in front of me. I'll then take some more photos of the print and of the room I've discovered, so you can see my description of them corresponds to reality.

13 April, 5 pm

How glad I am, dear Xabier, that I'm here on my own and you're far away! How glad I am to have given you a detailed account of these events in my letters! How else could I convey to someone other than you the horror I now feel, and which I suppose will accompany me the rest of my life? Who better than you could declare that this is not the fruit of a deranged mind?

Here, in front of me, is the print, which I examined less than an hour ago, intending to take some photos. You know what it was like just now, the side door wide open, as I described it to you at the start of this letter. Well, it's changed again! The whole room is as I last saw it, but now the side door is closed, as it was in the beginning. That's not what worries me, however, such changes are nothing new for me. What fills me with horror is what I saw or thought I saw – I swear I'm not dreaming – when I opened the book at the page with the print and noticed the door was closing right before me.

The fact the door was closing is not what fills me with horror. This just means, for the first time, I've witnessed the changes happening. What froze my blood, what chilled my senses, what sentenced me to this perpetual horror was briefly, in the space of a moment, seeing or thinking I saw part of... of the being, the animal or whatever it was closing the door from inside the small cell.

If I could find words to describe what my eyes observed, I'd be using them now. But it's beyond me. I don't know how to put into words what I saw, what has congealed my insides, what has left me like an animal whose last drop of blood has been sucked out of it. I'm so afraid my whole body is trembling in case the door in the print (not to mention the real door downstairs, next to the kitchen) should open again. I'm not even sure I'll be able to stay here this night. Because it occurs to me I'm still in time to take the car and drive to Pontedeume, to rent a room in the hotel and, early tomorrow morning, to flee this place, to flee this Galicia I should perhaps never have returned to.

And yet I sense there's something tying me to this house, I can't say what. I have the impression, even if my brain comes up with an escape plan, a stronger force lodged inside me is pulling on me to stay. And so I think my duty is to wait, to let the hours of this night go by, hours during which I know I will remain awake – how could anyone sleep after all that's happened? – waiting for the light of day.

Then I will enter the underground chamber, in search of whatever's hiding down there. I have no other choice. I cannot ignore this girl's plea for help, leave her in the hands of… this something, or someone, I dare not even imagine. I will take my revolver with me and won't hesitate to shoot any strange being I come across inside the crypt. If everything goes well, if everything goes as I desire, I'll send you another letter tomorrow with the results of my expedition. But if something should happen to me, if you see this letter is followed by no other, please come and rescue me as soon as you can. Bieito knows all about you, I've often told him about our friendship, he has a key for the house; don't hesitate to ask him for it in case of necessity.

I've no wish to go out, but must do so. I have to go to the Stuttgart, despite the terrible condition I'm in. I want to leave this letter I'm sending you now, because I'm afraid tomorrow I may no longer be able to. Something tells me the girl is in danger, what's happening beneath my feet, in that dark, unknown crypt, may be something terrible.

Farewell, my friend. I hope tomorrow to be sitting here again, telling you what is down below. The force pulling on me is stronger than my fear, I feel like the sailors on Ulysses' ship before the sirens' song. And I've forgotten to bring wax for my ears, nor are there ropes to tie me to the sanctuary of a mast. Why am I overcome by a sense that this is the end of everything?

Adrián

11

I suppose anyone still reading these pages does so after reading the letters Adrián sent me and seeing the photos which show the various changes to the print my friend described in such detail. So whoever is reading my words now knows as much as I did before I undertook the journey that brought me to this house. That means all I have to do is describe my movements after I read the letters, which shouldn't be difficult.

When I finished poring over Adrián's correspondence, I was deeply concerned. I have a taste for fantasy literature, my shelves are full of books dealing with these themes; one of my novels, *Conversation at Sunset*, could even be included in this genre. Adrián knew about this partiality of mine, which he never shared. Was all this an invention on his part because of the advert for a haunted house? Was it a clever scheme to force me to get in the car and drive to his new home? And yet this idea didn't fit in well with Adrián's character, he struck me as incapable of such jokes. Besides, there was something in his letters, especially in the last ones, which gave off a distinct air of authenticity. And then there were the photos, this unsettling record of the changes that took place in the print, though of course for an artist as extraordinary as my friend they wouldn't be difficult to manipulate.

Adrián's most recent letter was five days old. I believe there is no such thing as chance, there is always some dark reason for the things that befall us. If he was in trouble, it was a stroke of luck I should have come back right at that moment. I just needed time to throw some clothes and a few toiletries in a travelling bag, take the car and head in the direction of Vilarmaior.

The journey was easy enough. I took the motorway to Coruña and, at the Guísamo exit, joined the A6 towards Ferrol. As the magnificent Eume valley was opening out in front of me, a sign on the right indicated the turning for Vilarmaior. I took it and, after a couple of miles, there was a fork in the road, one branch of which led to the ancient Andrade Tower. I could glimpse it through the pines on the side of the road; it was in ruins, like most of the monuments in this country worth preserving. I carried on along the Vilarmaior road, which was narrow and bendy, so I had to drive slowly, and soon reached the village of Doroña.

I stopped in front of the old parish church, an excellent example of the popular Galician Romanesque style; the cemetery, two tall cypresses at the entrance, and a large, open area, presided over by a stately black acacia, rounded off this wonderful sight. I was admiring the simple beauty of the whole when I noticed a young woman pulling a cart full of grass up the road. I asked for the village of Breanca. She gave me very clear directions, and I soon found the place and the Stuttgart, situated by the road. I parked the car a short distance away, next to an old communal washing place, and entered the bar.

A man stood behind the counter. This had to be Bieito, who was familiar to me from reading Adrián's letters. I introduced myself and explained I'd come to stay with my friend for a few days. He answered they hadn't seen him in a while, perhaps he'd had to travel unexpectedly, though he found that strange. I noticed an unusual glint in his eyes, as if he wished to establish some sort of connection with me. But I wasn't going to share my misgivings with someone I barely knew, so I confessed I wasn't surprised, when Adrián was focused on a painting, he was capable of being stuck in his studio for more than a week. He seemed to accept my explanation and ended up saying he had a key for the house and Adrián had told him to give it to me, should I ever turn up asking.

I took the key and left the bar. Following his directions, I soon reached the building. It was even more beautiful than I'd imagined. There was something different about that house, in contrast with others in the area, which, apart from the odd atrocity erected by ignorant people, were typical rural dwellings for this part of the Mariñas. I say it was different because such colonial houses are to be found in the area around Ferrol, but they're always very close to the seashore. I remembered having been in one in Seixo a few years before, where an old girlfriend of mine used to live. But it was unusual to come across such a building in Vilarmaior, where the sea was just a blot on the horizon and everything pointed to the rustic lands of Monfero.

The shutters on most of the windows were closed, giving the impression the house was unoccupied, an impression that was reinforced by the reigning silence. I returned to the idea I'd had in the beginning, that this was all a joke by Adrián. I was surprised not to see my friend's car anywhere. Perhaps he had been called away, as the man in the bar had suggested, and would come back this day or the next. I was there now and felt the most obvious thing for me to do was to make myself at home and await his return. Inside the house, I might even find a note.

I got out of the car and stopped in front of the building, unable to avoid the memory of everything Adrián had said in his letters. I went up to the door, which was locked, opened it and entered the house. I called for Adrián, but got no answer. A quick look round the rooms downstairs confirmed everything was in order, there was no sign of anything untoward. The large living room was full of pictures, some of them finished, others still in progress. There was nothing out of place, just the things you would expect in the house of an active painter.

I went to the kitchen, eager to see what I would find. Here my hypothesis received its first confirmation. Because, had it been true what Adrián wrote in his letters, I would now be standing in front of a demolished wall, with an open room and floor covered in rubble. What met my eyes in the kitchen was something else. Everything was where it had to be and on the far side, where I might have expected the remains of a partition giving access to a concealed room, there was nothing other than a beautiful walnut sideboard, with crockery, glasses, bottles and other objects you would normally find in such a piece of furniture. I confess, when faced by proof that this was just a stratagem on Adrián's part, my heart was freed of its anguish. I noticed the kitchen walls had been freshly painted, the smell of paint in the air indicating the work had only recently been finished.

Feeling calmer now, I explored the rest of the ground floor, and the first floor as well, without encountering any oddities. On the landing I saw the trapdoor leading to the attic, at least this part of Adrián's story was true. I immediately felt curious and decided to take a closer look. I went downstairs to the storeroom, hoping to find the ladder Adrián had used, and there it was. I carried it up to the landing, pushed open the trapdoor with a stick, so I could position the ladder, and prepared to repeat the movements my friend had described in his letter.

When I entered the attic, it took my eyes a while to get used to the darkness, but then I could see everything was as my friend had said: the boxes, the trunk, the table... The table! I almost fell backwards, through the open trapdoor, when I realized there was a large book on the table. Had Adrián taken his joke this far?

I went over to the skylight and pulled back the blind, allowing the April sun to illuminate the furthest corners. I approached the table and started leafing through the book, overcome by nervousness. As I scanned the initial pages, I understood this was the book of prints my friend had talked about. A heaviness weighed on my chest as I turned the pages, like a dark premonition. And it happened, of course it happened, I suppose it was inevitable. As I turned another page, my eyes landed on the print I knew so well, a reproduction that was just as Adrián had described it the first time – a girl with her back to the spectator, leaning out of the window, gazing at a landscape I recognized immediately from what I already knew. Adrián hadn't lied about this, it really was the view from the north side of the house.

Would my friend's joke end here? Had he arranged all of this on the basis of facts, just as I do with my novels? I knew how to find out, of course I knew, but it made me afraid just to think about it. All I had to do was let a few hours go by and then re-examine the print in front of me. If it was the same, as

I expected, I would have definitive proof that this was just an ingenious scheme devised by my friend.

I emerged from the attic with the heavy book and decided, if I was going to stay, the first thing I had to do was make myself comfortable. I went to fetch my bag and searched for the room with the figure over the door Adrián had wanted me to have. It was a spacious bedroom, painted green, with a small balcony; the furniture was new and had clearly been arranged for guests. I then went down to the kitchen. I hadn't eaten for a while and my stomach was beginning to resent this fact. The fridge was full, so I quickly prepared an easy meal: fried eggs, chips and chorizos. It tasted wonderful, I was only sorry I didn't have any fresh bread.

Having finished and prepared some coffee, I cleared the table and placed the book of prints on it. As I searched for the page I wanted, my heart started thumping furiously and my chest contorted. With the print in front of me, a cold sweat invaded my body, my eyes even misted over. Because the image showed the same room and the same girl. But the girl had changed position and was now leaning against the window, staring at me, an earnestness in her expression, but also a touch of malice. The side door, which supposedly led to the tiny cell Adrián had talked about, was partially open.

I slammed the book shut and threw it on the kitchen floor. I didn't want to touch it, it horrified me to be in the same room as that accursed volume. Reacting irrationally, I left the house, crossed the garden and sat down under an old oak tree on the other side of the road, searching for sensations that would restore me to normality.

Little by little, I calmed down. I again felt lucid and tried to examine the things that had occurred to me. It was obviously not a joke. I could now be certain Adrián's story was true, at least regarding the strange properties of that book. I was clearly in front of something that defied logic and the rationalism of my mind. But I knew I'd come to Doroña in answer to Adrián's call for help. My friend was clearly in grave danger, faced by something I could scarcely imagine.

I went back into the house. I knew what I had to do, but curiosity got the better of me and, like Lot's wife, I again opened the book at the fateful page. The girl, who turned on me eyes full of anguish, was in the middle of writing a message on the wall. I could read the words 'HELP!' and 'XAB', the first three letters of my name. I slammed it shut. Let her write what she wanted! I wasn't going to be swayed by her suppliant eyes or pleas for help. I wasn't going to fall into the same trap as Adrián; I knew another task awaited me.

In the storeroom, I searched for the mallet my friend had used. I then returned with it to the kitchen. I almost broke my back moving the sideboard, which seemed made of lead rather than wood. As soon as I could, I started banging the wall with that mallet. It gave way easily, as I'd expected; the cement was fresh and hadn't had time to stick to the bricks, the work was only a few days old.

It was no surprise to me behind the partition to find the room Adrián had described. An empty room, with a blocked external window and a clearly visible side door. I jumped over the rubble and opened it, unable to wait any more. No surprises there either: the worrying iron trapdoor was in the centre of the room, with its engraving, the mysterious Labyrinth of Mogor. My friend hadn't recognized it, but I knew it well. I still remember the impression it made on me when, some years ago, I gazed on that strange rock-carving near the town of Marín, the vestige of a world so distant from our own.

I was just thinking about fetching a torch with which to illuminate the hole I expected to find under the trapdoor when I noticed something unusual. An irregular-shaped piece of cardboard propped against the wall, next to the door. I picked it up and returned to the light of the kitchen. There was writing on one side and, despite the scribbled letters, I knew it belonged to Adrián.

I sat down in a chair. Dusk was falling, so I had to make an effort to decipher what was written on that card. In unsteady letters written in pale red ink, I made out the following message:

> Dear Xabier,
> If you've got this far, then you must know the truth. But you may not have fallen into their traps, you may still be in time to save yourself. Abandon everything, Xabier, and leave. Go far away, where they cannot reach you!
> Don't look for me, I'm lost. If you caught sight of me now, you'd turn and run. To understand this, you'd have to see what I've seen, you'd have to know what is down here below. If I could find words to tell you what is inside this crypt, to tell you what I have become, you'd lose your mind. Go now, you're still in time. Go, and abandon what's left of me!

As I read these words, I heard a noise coming from the small cell. I stood up and went over to the door. From there, in the shady room, I saw someone lifting the trapdoor from inside and a shapeless bulk appearing out of the hole. I am grateful dusk had fallen and everything was dark, I am grateful I couldn't see clearly. The only thing I could make out, in that repulsive creature, was two bright eyes which seemed to transmit all the horror a human being can conceive. The eyes stared at me in a way I cannot describe. But it wasn't the look that made me mad, it wasn't this presence that made me run away and seek refuge in the room where I am now. No, what drove me crazy was the voice which continues to echo in my ears. A voice that seemed to emerge from unimaginable depths, a voice that exclaimed:

'Go, Xabier! They're hungry! Go, and don't come back.'

Because in these words, albeit horribly deformed – and this is what sent me over the edge – I was able to recognize the voice of my erstwhile friend, Adrián.

It's been two days since the events just related. Two days I've spent in this room I'm in, holding out thanks to the food I brought up from the kitchen, letting the hours go by without doing anything but breathe, as if my limbs were all paralyzed. Paralyzed, that's right, because that voice seems to have erased all thoughts from my mind and, in their place, I feel a horror I couldn't describe even if I wanted to, knowing now I'm faced by things that don't belong to the world we humans inhabit.

Of course I should have left before, when I was still in time. But I see there's no help for it and I won't be able to leave. A force is growing inside me, calling me, drawing me to enter the dark crypt underneath this house. I'm like an iron filing attracted by a powerful magnet. Something tells me I don't have long to go before joining Adrián.

Through the window I can hear Bieito's voice. I must tell him to wait for a moment. It was risky going down to the studio and phoning him, asking him to come, but it was the only way to make sure these documents arrived at their destination. I shall open the window now and ask him to post them. I shall put this letter I'm about to finish in an envelope together with my friend's letters and photos. I shall send everything to my sister, with instructions on what she has to do. This way at least I can try to avoid others being trapped as Adrián is at the moment, and I soon will be.

I'm not under any illusions, I know I can't put up much of a fight. I still have food for a few days, but last night I heard claws scratching at the door, I don't even want to imagine the creature they belong to. The door is thick, but I don't suppose it will withstand the onslaught many more nights. Should they come for me under cover of darkness, I'll confront the horror waiting on the other side. But should I see once more the light of dawn, perhaps I'll summon the strength for one final act: to go down to the crypt with the only weapon available to me – fire, purifying fire. People have made sacrifices with fire since time immemorial. If I have to die to save Adrián, to save myself, to save the whole of humanity, I'm ready. So now I shall bring this letter to a close, knowing what awaits me.

....

12

The fire that occurred on the night of 23-24 April, destroying the whole house, would not have received much space in the newspapers had it not been quickly linked to the disappearance of the famous painter Adrián Novoa and his friend Xabier Louzao, the internationally renowned Galician author. News about the violent fire and subsequent police investigation, reports on the two artists, articles about their respective works, filled the newspaper pages for several days, events that were closely followed on radio and TV.

On the afternoon of 23 April, Tareixa Louzao arrived at Vigo police station, where she spoke to Inspector Soutullo and showed him the documents in the envelope from her brother. The meeting was more positive than she'd expected. The inspector fully understood Tareixa's anxiety and the need to respond quickly. Having discussed the best course of action, they decided to drive to Doroña. The two of them wanted to know if there was any truth in the fantastical events related in those letters, or whether this was really nothing more than a joke by Xabier or the draft of a new novel in which, as so often, fiction and reality were mysteriously combined. Soutullo needed a few hours to see to some urgent matters, so they arranged to set out the following morning.

They left Vigo early. It was before 7 am when they joined the motorway at Isaac Perol junction and headed in the direction of Ferrol. They travelled in silence, allowing the radio to take the place of conversation. Tareixa concentrated on driving and, from time to time, glanced at the inspector, whose attention was drawn to the landscape.

As they were passing Padrón, they heard an announcement about the fire on the radio. The news flash simply mentioned a large fire in a house in Doroña parish and gave no further details. But, overwhelmed by what they'd just heard, both of them knew this had to be the house Adrián had bought, where Xabier had written the long message they'd read previously.

It wasn't difficult to reach Doroña, they followed the directions in the letters. The ancient Andrade Tower, the parish church, the communal washing place... Neither of them had ever been there, but both had the impression they were on familiar ground.

From where they parked the car, opposite the bar Stuttgart, they could see a thick column of grey smoke rising into the sky. Having walked to the house, which was surrounded by locals, they realized there was nothing they could do. The building contained a large amount of wood, which had caused the flames to spread. The fire had devoured everything, leaving only a few blackened beams. The roof had collapsed, as had part of the back wall. Only the rest of the outside walls and the occasional partition were still standing. From a distance, the house looked like the grimy skeleton of some prehistoric animal.

The firefighters from Ferrol had managed merely to stop the flames and make it safe to enter the building. The police officers who'd come to investigate the blaze found the charred remains of some furniture and other domestic objects, as well as books and pictures that had been reduced to ashes. But there was no sign of the two friends' bodies, which suggested they hadn't been in the house when the fire broke out. And yet the fact both their cars were still parked in a field opposite made it difficult to believe they'd left, unless they'd done so on foot or in another vehicle. The investigation soon confirmed the fire had started in the kitchen and may have been intentional; several burst petrol cans had been found to support this theory.

Tareixa and Inspector Soutullo introduced themselves and gave a statement. They kept quiet about the documents only they had seen, claiming they'd come to pay Xabier and Adrián a visit and unfortunately arrived the same day as the fire. Having obtained permission to enter what remained of the building, under the discreet gaze of one of the officers, they centred their attention on the search for evidence that would prove or disprove the truth of Adrián's strange letters and Xabier's lengthy explanation, which was not without its contradictions. Hadn't Xabier said, when he arrived, Adrián's car was nowhere to be seen? And yet there it was, parked a short distance from the house.

They decided to start looking in the kitchen, hoping to find answers to questions that didn't have any. Off the kitchen, as the letters said, was a small side room, which led to a reduced space that may have served as a pantry. There, if everything they'd read was true, would be the entry to the crypt.

On finding themselves alone in this cell-like space, they removed rubble, burnt wood, ashes and everything covering the floor. With a mixture of relief and disappointment, they saw there was no trapdoor, the cement floor was completely smooth. For some strange reason, Adrián and Xabier had lied about this crucial detail in their accounts.

They spent the whole day communicating with the authorities and chatting to the neighbours. At one point they thought it would be useful to have a look around the surroundings, using the fact Soutullo was a policeman to gain access. When night fell, aware there was nothing they could do until the following day, they drove to Pontedeume and rented rooms in the Hotel Eumesa, where Adrián had stayed several months earlier.

Unable to sleep, Tareixa kept going over the events of the last few days, trying to piece together a puzzle that didn't seem to make sense. She had full confidence in Soutullo, no one better than him to spot any evidence. But she felt her presence was also necessary, perhaps because only she really believed not everything was lost for Xabier and Adrián.

After a detailed investigation that lasted another two days, Soutullo came to the same conclusion as the authorities: neither Adrián Novoa nor Xabier Louzao could be declared dead, since there was no proof either of them had been in the house at the time of the fire. They were officially given as disappeared, which led various newspapers to come up with all sorts of ideas as to what had happened to the two artists. Given Adrián's eccentric character and the cosmopolitan life they were known for, it was entirely possible they were far away and would end up showing signs of life in the coming weeks.

Inspector Soutullo decided to return to Vigo, since there was nothing else he felt he could do in Doroña. He was a pragmatic man and refused to find answers where there weren't any. Tareixa, however, chose not to leave. She didn't believe these reports that struck her as meaningless.

She phoned the health centre and asked for a few more days off, given the circumstances. She then settled into her room in the hotel in Pontedeume, determined to find out the truth of what had happened to Xabier and her secret love, Adrián. She felt sure the letters and Xabier's description were not purely a literary device. She couldn't explain it, but for some reason she believed what was written in those documents, even though they referred to events that contravened the rudiments of logic and the laws governing this world.

As the days went by, the locals began to lose interest in the fire, avoiding the house and taking long detours so they wouldn't have to pass in front of it. They'd got used to the presence of Tareixa, who drove up to Breanca every day and spent hours wandering aimlessly in the surroundings of the burnt building, which seemed to pull on her, as an iron filing is drawn by a magnet, to use Xabier's words.

What's more, she sometimes had the impression something or someone was near her, a kind of dark, inexplicable presence. She'd be walking along some path and experience an intense feeling of danger, as if someone were behind her, meaning to do her harm. She would turn around, afraid, only to find again and again that she was completely alone. Or, as she herself thought, to find the presence following her movements wasn't human and was invisible to the eyes.

One afternoon she decided to visit the Crowns, an area where there were the remains of a buried Celtic camp. Myriad local legends were connected to this place, as she had been led to discover during long conversations in the bar

Stuttgart. Some of these legends seemed somehow related to the location of the house, which wasn't far away, and this made her want to explore the remains.

She soon arrived, using the directions she'd been given. Several mounds on the ground clearly indicated where the walls of houses in the camp were buried. Having examined the place, Tareixa sat down on a rock which rose from the earth like the upper part of a monolith. She gazed out at the surrounding hills covered in pines and eucalyptuses, though patches of lighter green showed where the original forest had stood its ground. It was a stunning afternoon, the sky streaked with the reds of sunset. She'd always been told the ancient Celts built their camps in high places to defend themselves from enemies, but it occurred to her they'd done so as well to contemplate the beauty of the earth they inhabited, the vast spectacle of life going on in front their eyes.

At one particular moment she thought she saw something strange on the ground, next to a clump of broom. She stood up and went to see what it was that had caught her attention. She took the object in her hands and noticed it was a large leather-bound volume burnt around the edges. She'd never seen it before, but knew at once what it was; her heart was beating fast even before she read the title. It was obviously the book of prints Adrián and Xabier had written about. How had it got there, to this place half a mile from the house?

Controlling her nerves, she began to turn the scorched pages, carefully examining the prints and waiting to come across the one she knew so well after seeing Adrián's photos. She wondered if in the image of the room and girl she would find some clue as to the others' disappearance.

She finally reached the sheet she had been looking for. There was no doubt this was the room from the photos, though what met her eyes was not at all what she'd expected. Tareixa believed she was prepared for anything, but the sight of the print paralyzed her brain and filled her with fear. She felt dizzy and dropped the book, reaching for the rock to steady herself. The pieces of the puzzle suddenly slotted into place, and she realized her presence there was no longer necessary.

She knew now what she had to do, as if some inner voice were dictating her movements. She was convinced there was a strong link between that accursed volume and the unknown forces hiding in the crypt. If that was the case, if the book helped these forces to reach the outside world, something told her it might also serve for their destruction.

She took the book and marched towards the car, which was parked near the house. She then opened the boot and found the envelope with all of Xabier's correspondence. She rummaged around and also found the firelighters she used when camping.

With all of this, she entered the ruins of the house and went straight to the spot where, judging by the letters, the trapdoor had to be that gave access to the underground staircase leading to the crypt. She swept away all the ash until the floor was clean. She then went out and fetched dry leaves, sprigs of broom, ferns, sticks, anything she thought would burn easily. She also took some old newspapers she kept on the back seat of the car.

She then drew a circle in the middle of the room and, having marked these limits, piled the kindling into a large pyramid, making sure the firelighters were at the base. When everything was ready, she took a match and lit one of the firelighters. The flames quickly spread to the rest of the pile.

Tareixa fed the fire with more sticks that were lying about until she had a good bonfire with plenty of embers. Then without hesitating, with the sense of determination that had overcome her half an hour earlier, she threw the book of prints and her brother's envelope, with all its documents, on top of the fire. At first it seemed the book wouldn't burn and might even smother the flames but, little by little, the flames overcame any resistance, and the book and documents began to be swallowed up.

Tareixa may already have been expecting this because she wasn't surprised when the ground began to shake and cracks appear in the cement floor, as if something underground were about to break. At the same time, a cold breeze suddenly arose, making her shiver as if she were naked on a winter's day. The leaves of the nearest trees rustled violently and the dogs in the neighbouring houses started howling. An underground rumble, which seemed to emerge from the depths of the earth, grew until it was unbearable, deafening her to such an extent she thought her eardrums were going to burst. But Tareixa didn't move, she thought about nothing, rooted to the spot like a menhir, gazing obsessively at the flames spiralling in the air, until everything she had thrown on the fire was reduced to ashes. At that point, the noise, the tremors, the cold air reached a maximum and then quickly disappeared. Silence and calm regained control of the afternoon.

When everything had finished, Tareixa left the ruins and walked to the car. She was convinced she had finally fulfilled her purpose, sure now that the curse hidden in the house was well and truly beaten, and no one else would ever have to confront that same horror.

She got in the car and pulled away. She didn't look back. She knew she was at the start of a long journey, a journey that would take her back to the real world, away from a world she had never suspected existed. Her hands clasping the steering wheel, her eyes fixed on the road, she felt nothing would ever be the same. She knew she would never see Adrián and Xabier again in the land of the living. But she trusted they might at least both rest in peace for the whole of eternity.

Read more titles in the series  published by Small Stations Press!

Agustín Fernández Paz, BLACK AIR

Had I remained silent, had I concealed my interest at that point, I might now be in a completely different situation, far away from the horror that has been ceaselessly gnawing away at me for the past three years. And yet my words simply paved the way for what Dr Montenegro had to say:

'You will learn more about Laura Novo, Dr Moldes. She is going to be your first patient. Under my supervision, of course. You have new ideas, you may be the only person capable of shedding light on a case that has kept the rest of us in the dark. I know it's not an easy challenge, but perhaps, with your passion for knowledge, you're the only one who can find a solution that goes beyond the boundaries of accepted practice. I'll have her case history sent to you at once. Good luck, Víctor, my friend, and welcome to Beira Verde Clinic!'

Víctor Moldes is an outstanding psychiatry student, looking to test his knowledge on patients. He is given a job at the prestigious Beira Verde Clinic in Galicia, near the Portuguese border, and handed a patient, Laura Novo, who is capable only of writing her name on blank sheets of paper. Slowly he draws her out of herself and she agrees to tell him her story, how she left Madrid in order to work on her thesis and escape a difficult relationship that was going nowhere. Her return to the land where she grew up, to stay in a guest house run by a schoolteacher she had fallen passionately in love with when she was a teenager, has fatal consequences. Her presence in the remote area of Terra Chá awakens the Great Beast, who up until that moment had been slumbering in the depths of the earth. Once awake, the Great Beast has one year to achieve its objective. Dr Moldes finds himself drawn into a conflict he is barely able to understand, let alone control, and, having finally pieced together the fragments of the narrative, he is in a race against time to save his patient.

ISBN 978-954-384-028-1

Fina Casalderrey, DOVE AND CUT THROAT

'Yeah, I like birds, so what? Just because I have a thing about them, don't believe it, that's another story. There's stuff that won't let me sleep, I'm warning you. Recently I've started getting up at night, going to the kitchen, grabbing the sharpest knife I can find and then heading straight for the exit with the aim of sticking the knife in the chest of whoever has hurt me at some point in my life. I have to be restrained because I'm out of my mind. There are times I even have to be tied with ropes until I calm down, just in case I succumb to another fit... I want you to know that accepting my friendship means belonging to a high-risk group because, I'm telling you, when I fly off the handle...'

I had to intimidate them somehow. School had turned into a place where I was failing on a daily basis. Every morning, when I went in, I looked at those walls and felt like running away, as if from fire. Putting up with all the abuse day after day was pretty hard, and there was no way I was going to bother my mother with all that nonsense. I quickly realized that at school it was your appearance that mattered.

André Santomé Lobeira is a teenager whose parents divorced when he was five. He puts on a front at school to defend himself against the bullies Raúl Pernas and Héctor Solla, who do everything they can to make his life miserable. He starts deliberately getting low marks in the hope they will ignore him. This encourages his grandfather to intervene, and André goes to live with his grandparents, who run a restaurant, *The Birdhouse,* in the garden of which his grandfather has an orphanage for birds. André finds a baby cut-throat finch, a finch with a red line across its neck, and keeps it as a pet. He is torn between two girls — Halima, a Moroccan girl in his class whose mother died as they were crossing into Spain, who helps him stand up to the bullies; and Dove, a girl he meets on the Internet, who helps him with his homework and when his grandfather falls ill. Dove arranges for them to meet in person, but André is afraid this will ruin their friendship and feels a strange sense of betrayal to the other girl in his life, Halima. He almost wishes Dove had never arranged their meeting...

ISBN 978-954-384-029-8

Marcos Calveiro, THE PAINTER WITH THE HAT OF MALLOWS

'The night is a lot more alive. You can see colours better than during the day,' Vincent had told me.

Adeline and I, sitting on the ground very close to each other, watched him paint under the moonlight. He had a small candle attached to the brim of his hat and had placed two bigger candles on the easel to illuminate the canvas, where he was releasing brushstrokes with the same burning enthusiasm as always.

I was afraid at some stage the wax might melt and Vincent would burn himself or cause a fire in the field where we were sitting, but he carried on talking and painting without a rest. I still couldn't believe I was there in Adeline's company, alone under the night sky, surrounded by sheaves of wheat.

When Vincent told me he planned to go on a nocturnal expedition, I was very surprised.

A teenage boy is sent by his mother to spend a few days in the country as a way of getting him out of trouble. In the town of Auvers-sur-Oise, one hour north of Paris, the boy finds life with his great-aunt unbearable — that is until the arrival of the painter Vincent van Gogh, who has come to escape difficulties in the south. It is the summer of 1890 and already eight months have passed since the boy left his mother. He begins a friendship with the painter, taking him to places he hasn't seen and engaging in conversations that open his eyes to a different way of viewing the world, bringing to an end his turbulent past. He also struggles with the reasons for his mother's disappearance from the town where she grew up and experiences the first embers of romantic love when he develops an interest in the daughter of van Gogh's innkeeper, Adeline. Based on real events, this imaginative story of a teenage boy's friendship with an inspired painter and participation in the events of a provincial town, where he meets the local doctor, a war hero, and railway pointsman, as well as the man who could turn out to be his real father, rushes to its inevitable conclusion like the trains that slice through the countryside on their way to Paris.

ISBN 978-954-384-030-4

Elena Gallego Abad, DRAGAL I: THE DRAGON'S INHERITANCE

'Have a look around you, with wide open eyes. The catacombs are not far from here, but you have to be the one to find the keys. I shan't be able to accompany you on the last stage of your journey, I'm getting too old for such adventures, so I must fulfil my role as guide by getting you to come up with the correct answers. When it's time, the result will depend on your choices. And don't forget the search for the dragon will be worthless if you lose what matters to you most along the way.'

The priest spoke slowly and the boy began to feel desperate. Father Xurxo didn't seem prepared to give him the indications he needed and impatience was gnawing away at his soul.

'Please…'

The vicar took an apple out of his pocket, wiped it on the sleeve of his jacket and sat on a pew in the first row, gesturing to the boy to sit down beside him.

'Have a look around you, with wide open eyes, and tell me what you see,' he said again, biting into the fruit.

After the death of his father in a caving accident, Hadrián is forced to move to Galicia with his mother and start at a new school. His mother gives him a medallion that belonged to his father, showing a dragon in a threatening posture on one side and the same dragon incubating an egg on the other. When the dragon's tails move, the boy realizes this is no ordinary medallion. Meanwhile, he has noticed the stone effigy of a dragon on the cornice of St Peter's Church, which winks at him and infiltrates his thoughts. The boy's destiny, it seems, is to sacrifice himself so that the dragon can come back to life after an interval of a thousand years, during which it has been protected in the catacombs under the church. The boy and his classmate Mónica will first have to locate the catacombs with the help of the parish priest, Father Xurxo, before they can ascertain whether the dragon's existence is for real.

ISBN 978-954-384-031-1

Rosa Aneiros, I LOVE YOU LEO A. DESTINATION SOMEWHERE

Leo went through the security archway with far too much insecurity in her feet and restless pumping in her heart. That may be why the civil guard ordered her to take off her boots and passed the metal detector over her nervous body. Had it been able to measure her heartbeat, that little device would most probably have exploded as soon as it reached her chest. But it didn't explode, possibly because such instruments know nothing about the comings and goings of the soul. Meanwhile, the X-ray machine was closely examining the contents of her rucksack. The rucksack didn't seem exactly comfortable with its contents. It had gone from carrying sheets, folders, books and notes to holding lists of Internet addresses, descriptions in different languages, a passport, a brand-new debit card, some socks and a scarf.

After university, Leo is due to go travelling for six months with her friends Aldara, Inés and Martiño, but at the last minute her friends pull out and Leo is left to travel on her own. Her first stop, in Lisbon, Portugal, is a rain-soaked disaster. She is dragged around the city by her overbearing host and only really gets a feel for the city during the final few days, when she is cooped up in his apartment. But everything changes with her next destination, Barcelona, where she meets up with a group of friends from Latin America who call themselves 'Ruth & Co.' and busk for a living. Romance, excitement, frustration, appalling and luxurious living conditions, familiar and foreign cultures, follow as Leo travels to Granada, Córdoba, Seville and Cádiz in Andalusia, Marrakesh in Morocco and finally Istanbul. In this first instalment of Leo's travelling adventures, Leo discovers that she must learn how to leave a place before she can truly enjoy her experiences, and how travelling can bring you back full circle. She is also mystified by the graffiti that keeps appearing along her route: 'I Love You Leo A.' Who is it that has scrawled this graffiti wherever she goes, and what do they want? Only by continuing with her journey and not giving up will Leo find out the answer to this riddle!

ISBN 978-954-384-040-3

Elena Gallego Abad, DRAGAL II: THE DRAGON'S METAMORPHOSIS

'About fifty years ago, towards the start of the 1960s, an old priest on his deathbed gave his deacon a wooden box, charging him never to open it... until he received a sign from the stone statue affixed to the façade of St Peter's. He then revealed that he belonged to a secret order whose duty it was to protect a dragon's magic and prepare its return to life.'

'A knight of the Order of Dragal!'

'The task didn't seem all that difficult. He should never open the box or mention it to anybody... All he had to do was wait for signs that would herald the fulfilment of a thousand-year-old prophecy.'

'Have you been waiting all this time?'

Father Xurxo nodded...

In this second instalment of the saga by Elena Gallego Abad devoted to the Galician dragon Dragal, the schoolboy Hadrián, who with his friend Mónica discovered the dragon's remains in the catacombs under St Peter's Church, is locked in a struggle with the dragon to see who will come out on top. Mónica has promised to take some food to the Moor's Pool, where her friend has gone for refuge, but is unsure what dragons eat when they're not devastating the local population. Before setting out, however, she receives strange, handwritten messages of warning, telling her not to go. She seeks help — first from the parish priest, Father Xurxo, who produces an ancient box containing three objects that might be the Grand Master's keys, and then from a police officer, Cortiñas, who turns out to have a vested interest in the dragon's well-being. When Hadrián goes missing, his mother calls the police, but only Mónica knows where he really is. Will she inform the police and break her promise not to reveal where he is hiding? If she does, will the police be in time to save her friend, and what will become of the dragon he has started to turn into?

ISBN 978-954-384-042-7

Read more Galician literature in English published by Small Stations Press!

Fiction:

Xurxo Borrazás, VICIOUS

Álvaro Cunqueiro, FOLKS FROM HERE AND THERE

Miguel-Anxo Murado, SOUNDCHECK: TALES FROM
THE BALKAN CONFLICT

Manuel Rivas, ONE MILLION COWS

Suso de Toro, POLAROID

Poetry:

Rosalía de Castro, GALICIAN SONGS

Xosé María Díaz Castro, HALOS

Celso Emilio Ferreiro, LONG NIGHT OF STONE

Pilar Pallarés, A LEOPARD AM I

Lois Pereiro, COLLECTED POEMS

Manuel Rivas, FROM UNKNOWN TO UNKNOWN

For an up-to-date list of our publications, please visit
www.smallstations.com

For more information on Galician literature in English, please visit
www.galicianliterature.com